Celtic Mytho Illustrated fc Beginners

CW00504599

STONEHENGE

MEGALITES

MYTHOLOGY

"Do not separate your heart from the tongue, and all your actions will be successful."
(Amenmope)

Summary:

CONTENTS:

Mythology is an integral part of
human civilization, and in
Celtic mythology, in particular,
Western culture has its roots,
so much so that artists and
thinkers continue to read the
condition and events of
contemporary man against the
backdrop of Celtic myth. From
the eighteenth century onwards
this immense patrimony has

been the subject of an organic scientific discipline, which is intertwined with the study of anthropology, ethnography, psychoanalysis, literature, art, philosophy. In this volume a clear, concise and rigorous introduction to the knowledge of Celtic mythology is presented. Starting from the possible definitions of the myth, the work proposes a typology of myths exposed in a simple way for everyone, then illustrating the interpretations developed by the Celtics themselves.

STONEHENGE

The most famous of the stone buildings, the very symbol of European megalithic culture, is Stonehenge. It is located on Salisbury Plain (Wiltshire), in the south of England. Stonehenge is a cromlech, that is, a circle of stones. In reality, only a colossal fragment of the overall circular structure remains, because in the Middle Ages the monoliths of Stonehenge were used to construct buildings, and have thus disappeared.

The outermost circumference is a deep moat, about 100 meters in diameter, which delimits an embankment in which 56 wells have been dug, called Aubrey Holes,

"Aubrey's holes", named after the archaeologist who discovered them in 1666.

Proceeding inwards, there are other holes, arranged in a double semicircle. And here are the mighty monoliths, each of which weighs from 30 to 50 tons.

The external group, called Sarsen Circle, "circle of Sarsen", from the name of the stone in which the monoliths were carved, gray sandstone harder than granite, has a diameter of about 30 meters.

The 16 vertical slabs, almost

6 meters high, are surmounted by 6 architraves. Double in height are the triliths (i.e. 2 vertical monoliths with an architrave) of the even more internal structure, which reach 10 meters.

Between the two colonnades are placed the Bluestones, "blue stones", and in the center of the structure lies the Altar Stone, "altar stone", 5 meters long; on the outside there is the 7-meter Slaughter Stone, "stone of sacrifice" and, in the driveway leading to the monument, the Heel (or Hele)

Stone, "heel stone". Although incomplete, and largely destroyed, the colossal architecture of Stonehenge has kept its charm intact through the millennia.

It can be seen from afar, in the undulating valley in which it rises, solitary and silent.

Its blue stones come from the Prescelly Mountains, in Pembrokeshire, 300 kilometers from Stonehenge, and the Sarsen monoliths have been transported for at least 30 kilometers, from the quarries of the Marlborough Downs:

how was it possible to drag and raise such large and heavy stone boulders, with the technical means available in a prehistoric society, in which the use of the wheel was not known?

What could have pushed the architects of Stonehenge, like those of the countless European megalithic structures, to conceive such grandiose and so difficult works?

Such tiring work as the

raising of the large and heavy Monoliths had to arise from pressing needs, of a practical or magical, ritual or religious nature. As with prehistoric paintings and sculptures, megalithic constructions such as Stonehenge and Carnac have also aroused perplexity among scholars, who have long debated their meaning.

MEGALITES

The European territory is littered with spectacular and enigmatic megalithic creations. The number of such imposing stone monuments is very high and there are numerous sites that are little known to the general public, but which have nothing to envy to the most famous and best-used tourist locations.

Megaliths are, as the name implies, structures made up of enormous stones; in fact the expression derives from the Greek megas, large, and lithos, stone. They can have different shapes and structures, however, essentially, we can reduce all megaliths to some fundamental types that we will examine in detail. The simplest and most widespread megalith is the Menhir, a rough or roughly hewn stone set in the ground.

The name derives from the Breton men (stone) and hir (long). However, locally, other expressions may survive to indicate them, such as the archaic peulven, widespread in Brittany, or the term monk, used in Corsica. There are many types of Menhirs, of different sizes, functions and shapes. Some may have a height of a few decimeters, others can stand on the ground for about ten meters. The

Grand Menhir Brisé, located in Brittany, is currently demolished and broken into four parts, but originally it must have exceeded twenty meters in height.

There are still standing Menhirs of considerable height: the English one of Bridlington

(Yorkshire) of 7.5 meters, and the Breton one of Kerolas (Finistère), which exceeds 12 meters.

The name of stele is attributed to a large and thin standing stone, often worked and decorated. The Stelae are defined anthropomorphic when they are worked in such a way as to present a profile that wants to represent a human figure. The name of alignment is reserved for a series of Menhirs, or more rarely of steles, arranged in one or more rows. The best known names are the Breton ones, but they exist in Scotland, Ireland, Sardinia and Valle d'Aosta.

Sometimes the Menhirs are arranged in a circle, in a semicircle or in an ellipse, and then the name of Cromlech is attributed to this structure. The name comes from the Breton croum, curve, and lech, sacred stone. The largest is that of Avebury (Wiltshire) which has a diameter of over 360 meters. The most well-known Italian is that of the Valle d'Aosta pass of the Piccolo San Bernardo. Sometimes the Cromlechs can have straight sides, as in the case of the rectangular one of Crocune (Brittany).

The second basic type of megalith is the Dolmen. A Dolmen is made up of several slabs: a certain number of them are driven into the ground, so as to support one or more roofing boards. In its simplest form it is made up of three vertical plates (pillars, or orthostats) that support a fourth (table). The name comes from the Breton dol, table, and men, stone.

Dolmens can also be very

elaborate. Some have a series of vertical slabs, side by side and of reduced height, which lead to the chamber of the actual dolmen: these slabs are given the name of corridor. Others may have smaller side chambers, whether or not they are connected to the main chamber. The plan of a dolmen can take different shapes: in the simplest case it is square or rectangular, but there are dolmens with non-parallel sides, others that have a complex plan, others that are bent at an elbow, a detail that makes one suspect the existence of different moments of realization of the work.

Locally, the term Dolmen can be replaced by the expression dyser, in Denmark, mamra or anta in Portugal, tola or table in Corsica. Generally the corridor of a dolmen is narrower than the room, but in the case in which the corridor and the room are not differentiated, the name of allée couverte is attributed to the Megalith. There are also megalithic structures formed simply by a slab fixed vertically in the ground, on which the end of another large slab is placed: the name of semidolmen is reserved for a structure of this type. Above the dolmens a large circular embankment was often built, which is given the name of tumulus. If the roof was instead ensured by a pile of stones, often regular and well squared, then we speak of cairn, but it must be admitted that often the expressions mound and cairn are used with a certain ease, almost as synonyms. The Dolmens were sometimes made in pairs or in groups, covered or not by mounds. It should be remembered that megalithic structures were rarely built individually. Thus we find ourselves in the presence of large megalithic areas in which Menhirs, Dolmens and alignments are identified, generally gathered in a single sacred area.

Sometimes they were linked by specific meanings, often of an astronomical nature. Recently, in fact, archaeoastronomy, a science that studies the knowledge of astronomy of ancient populations, and the relative connections with the religious and social life of the time, has allowed us to understand that often the directions identified by megaliths (an alignment or axis of a Dolmen, for example) were anything but random and instead indicated some points on the horizon in which particular astronomical phenomena occurred.

The most common orientations concerned the points of rising or setting of the sun on particular dates, such as the equinoxes and solstices, or the extreme points reached by the moon in its complex motion. Thus the Megaliths were, at times, used as real astronomical observatories; at other times, however, they were oriented towards particular points of the horizon for ritual dying. In fact, in ancient times, a sort of astral religion had slowly been built. Naturally, astronomical interpretations do not take anything away from traditional hypotheses.

A Menhir could evidently

have a territorial significance, delimiting an area in which the group dominated. It could also represent a sort of commemorative monument, indicate the site of a battle, or it could be an object of worship. Even in the Middle Ages, many megaliths were attributed specific abilities and sometimes real rites were celebrated in their vicinity. Furthermore, it is undeniable to attribute a widespread funerary use to the dolmens. The importance of megalithic structures emerges even more forcefully when one thinks of the technical efforts that required realizations of this magnitude.

The pillars of Stonehenge, for example, were transported from more than 40 kilometers away, a cyclopean work for the time. In Europe there are some areas in which megaliths are particularly numerous or spectacular, but there are also lesser known places, in which surprising structures are found that are certainly worth a visit. Thus, when we speak of France, it is natural to think of Brittany, when instead the

French department that represents the largest number of menhirs, almost half a thousand, is the distant Aveyron.

Finally, it must be remembered that in the past megaliths were considered the work of fairies or giants and the home of dwarves or other fantastic beings. Thus the undeniable charm of these millenary stones adds to the halo of legend that surrounds them and which is often still alive in the local traditions of some areas. Before the scientific world recognized the prehistoric nature of megaliths, they were attributed to the Romans or the Celts, as evidenced by the name of some monuments, such as the Cordon des Druides (Fougères).

MYTHOLOGY

Caesar tells us how the druids used to instruct the scions of the clans; a similar remark is also present in Irish mythology, in numerous texts. It is possible that they taught with the help of epic verses; the students were therefore called to understand the messages that were hidden there, but this, also given the complexity of their metaphors, was not simple: two passages taken from different versions of Tain Bo Cualinge are witnesses of this. In one it is stated that Cathbad the Druid taught "more than a hundred amazed people" while in the other it is noted that only "eight of them were capable in the Druidic sciences". The allegories of their language were therefore not easily understood. In these texts, presumably the same ones that are handed down to us in the form of heroic epics, there were present in bulk "history, theology, philosophy, mythology, law, customs, prophecies.

Celtic mythological symbols of animals

Grammar, geography, etymology above all are not absent, but what is most striking in this tradition […] is the refusal to separate myth from history. Contrary to the Romans, the Celts thought their history mythically and, of course, they sometimes historicized their myths "(Jean Markale).

" That said, it is possible that the Druids voluntarily made their tales obscure, first to be understood only by those who could understand them, and then to better make a selection among those who knocked on the door of the Druid class ". Diodorus Siculus writes about the druids in this regard:" They speak little in their conversations, they express themselves in enigmas and in their language they do so as to let most things be guessed. They use hyperbole a lot, both to brag themselves and to belittle others. In their speeches they are menacing, haughty and drawn to the tragic. They are nevertheless intelligent and able to educate themselves. "

The epic tales handed down in greater quantity - and, above all, quality - are those of the

Irish epic cycle, structured in turn in different sections.

It is thanks to the patient transcription work of the Christian scribe monks that we have come into possession of these texts, which have also undergone inevitable alterations from the original form by their hand; the centralizing vision of the

Catholic Church has caused notable changes in parts considered superstitious or immoral, but overall the Irish works are still the "purest" ones in our hands, if compared for example with the Welsh Mabinogion, which has undergone considerable and heavy influences both on the part of the Church and on the part of medieval "courteous" literature, becoming more like the novels of Chretien de Troyes than a true Celtic epic.

As already mentioned, mythology, in addition to the

function of mere entertainment, was probably a sort of hermetic way of transmitting the druidic principles, from religion, to law, to poetics, to all the other numerous fields of teaching included in druidism. It is therefore obvious that some myths cannot be fully understood outside a purely Celtic, and in particular Druidic, point of view.

Irish mythology, due to the vastness of topics and information it contains, constitutes one of the major documents in our possession regarding Celtic society. We can draw from it numerous insights on different historical and social spheres. We will now address the major epic cycles, albeit in a much more general way than they deserve.

IDEAS FOR MORE INFORMATION:

Celtic mythology is the collection and therefore the study of Celtic myths belonging to the religious culture of the ancient Celtics and concerning, in particular, their gods and heroes. The Celtic myths were collected in cycles concerning the different areas of the Celtic world. The only unifying element is the composition of divine figures that also represent the forces or aspects of nature. Contemporary scholars study and analyze ancient myths in an attempt to shed light on the political and religious institutions and civilization. It consists of a large collection of tales explaining the origin of the world and detailing the life and adventures of a large number of gods and goddesses, heroes and heroines and other mythological creatures. These stories were initially composed and disseminated only in an oral poetic and compositional form.

So there are, all over the world, countless variations and authors to draw from.

Thank you...
Thank you...
Thank you...

CPSIA information can be obtained
at www.ICGtesting.com
Printed in the USA
BVHW040302280421
605952BV00015B/2431